Dedication

This book is dedicated to all readers,
both young and young at heart.

Oscar
The Christmas Kitten

A STORY OF HOPE

By

Robert & Beverly Kynor

Text and illustrations copyright 2010

by FHL Publishing

www.oscarkitten.com

The illustrations were created with pencil and watercolor and scanned digitally.

First Edition
October 2010

Library of Congress Control Number 2010928242

ISBN-978-0-9827087-0-5

Printed in U.S.A.

Manufactured by BookMasters, INC.
30 Amberwood Parkway, Ashland, OH 44805
Job Number: M7612

Oscar lived with his family in a house that was warm and cozy and full of love. It was early in December, and the house looked so pretty, all ready for Christmas.

He was not very big and he was not very old, but Oscar knew all about Christmas. He knew about the tree with the twinkling lights and the colorful ornaments.

He knew about the shining star at the top of the tree, and he knew about the joyful songs of Christmas. Most of all, Oscar knew about the love of his family and of Baby Jesus, and he was very happy.

Oscar liked to sit on the windowsill where he could see other houses with bright, sparkly lights. He thought to himself, "It sure would be fun to go visit those houses ."

Later that day, when his dad opened the front door to turn on their Christmas lights, Oscar ran outside.

He walked along the street looking at all the sparkling red and green lights, and thought that this was a very special time of year.

But Oscar was not very big, and he was not very old. The sky was getting dark, and it was so very cold. Oscar wanted to go home to his own warm and cozy house.

He said to himself, "I'm getting so tired, I need to rest for awhile." So Oscar climbed under a car to take a little nap.

Just as he fell asleep, the car started to move! Oscar was scared and climbed up by the engine. He held on tight as the car drove through the dark, cold night. The car ride seemed to last forever, bouncing along in the cold, winter weather.

Finally, the car stopped, and Oscar jumped off and ran behind a tree. "Where is my house?" thought Oscar.

"Where is my family?" But he was not very big and not very old and Oscar did not know which way to go to get home.

As he sat shivering under the tall pine tree, Oscar could hear voices calling his name. "Oscar, Oscar, where are you?" they said.

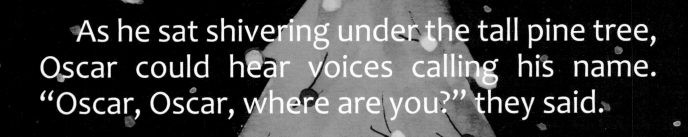

But the sky was dark, and it was getting so cold. As Oscar lay down by the tree, all he could think about was his warm, cozy bed.

The next morning, Oscar started walking again. "I want my family, I want to be with my friends," he said.

But Oscar was not very big and he was not very old and he did not know which way to go to get home. He went past big houses and little houses too. Oh, which way to walk, he wished he knew!

Sometimes a nice boy or girl would take him inside. They would give him some food, a soft bed, and a gentle rub on his soft, furry head.

But they were not his family. The house was not his warm, cozy home, so Oscar would leave and keep walking and looking, again all alone.

Day after day, Oscar searched for his home. Once more he heard voices calling his name. He even saw signs that said "Missing gray kitten—fluffy and friendly " Oscar thought to himself, "That sounds like me!"

Then he sighed, "When will I ever see my family?"

It was getting closer to Christmas, and Oscar was feeling sadder and sadder. "I hope Dad finds me soon," he thought. "I want to be with my own family in my warm, cozy home. It's been so dark and cold, and now it's starting to snow."

A nice lady walked by as Oscar sat down to rest. She said, "Why, you look like the kitten on the sign. You're gray and fluffy, and you look very friendly to me."

Then the nice lady picked Oscar up and held him tight, telling him, "I will call the number on the sign. I know you will be happy to be back with your family."

Soon, a shiny, white car drove up and stopped. Out stepped a tall man, calling Oscar's name. It was Oscar's dad! He had found his lost kitten at last.

So it was that Oscar, who was not very big and not very old and no longer alone, would now spend Christmas with his own family, in his own home.

At last he was back in his warm, cozy house with the pretty tree and the shining lights and the joyful songs. As he sat in the windowsill looking out at all the Christmas lights, he thought to himself, "This is truly a special season," and he was happy again.

AFTERWORD

This book is based on the true story of Oscar the kitten. Oscar was six months old at the time he set out on his amazing journey. He really did ride under a car for ten miles to a church parking lot, where he finally jumped off. It was early December, and during the three weeks that Oscar was missing, our hometown of Colorado Springs, Colorado, experienced some of the coldest and snowiest days in our city's history.

Oscar's extended human family and friends braved the cold weather and searched for him every day. Hundreds of flyers were passed out door to door and taped to telephone poles and street signs in hopes that someone would find him. Still, Oscar walked many blocks, crossing a number of busy streets, always heading south in the direction of his home.

We never gave up hope that Oscar would be reunited with his family. After all, kittens are one of God's creations, and He loves all his creatures, great and small. It is no coincidence that Oscar's journey took place near Christmas. As you know, it is the season for miracles.

About the Authors

A dynamic mother and son team, Beverly and Robert Kynor are both natives of Colorado. They share a love of teaching, music, children and, most of all, animals and their amusing antics.

Robert, a Summa Cum Laude graduate of Regis University, earned his degree in Elementary Education with special emphasis in children's literature. He was the recipient of the "Golden Apple," the prestigious award given to the outstanding Student Teacher of his class.

Beverly retired from teaching after enjoying nearly 40 years with elementary-aged children. One of her favorite classroom activities was "story time" where she could share her enjoyment of books with her students.

Both are avid readers, and lifelong learners. As accomplished musicians, the authors have performed on piano and guitar for a variety of audiences. Beverly has performed with the Pueblo, Colorado Symphony Orchestra as well working with school musical performing groups. Robert performs in a band and teaches private guitar lessons as well as running pickyouraxe.com, a handcrafted wood guitar pick business.

This is their first book together.

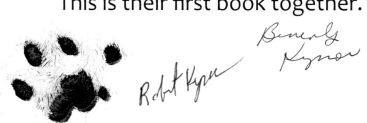

Robert & Beverly Kynor